EGMONT

We bring stories to life

First published in Great Britain 2012 by Dean,
an imprint of Egmont UK Limited
239 Kensington High Street, London W8 6SA

HiT entertainment

ISBN 978 0 6035 6679 0
51291/1
Printed in China

Carnival of Junk

It was early in the morning in Pontypandy. Mike Flood and his wife Helen were having breakfast. They were both very excited about going on holiday to Jamaica.

Mike began playing the drums on his teapot using his knife and fork.

"Tomorrow, I'll be playing this on the beach under the Caribbean sun," he dreamed.

There was a third place laid at the table for their daughter Mandy.

"Mandy!" called Helen. "Breakfast is ready!"

Mandy came downstairs and walked into the kitchen. Her face was covered in red spots!

"Mandy!" cried Helen in surprise. She quickly inspected Mandy's face, arms and chest.

"Chicken pox," Helen sighed. "You can't go anywhere for at least a fortnight."

"But, Mum!" cried Mandy. "What about our holiday to Jamaica? We were going to go to the carnival!"

"We'll just have to wait until next year," said Helen, putting her arm around Mandy as she led her daughter back upstairs.

Outside the Fire Station, the officers were having a training exercise with their metal-cutting equipment, the Jaws of Life.

Elvis' arm was stuck in some metal railings and Sam and Penny were using the tool to free him.

"This was meant to be a practice, Cridlington," boomed Station Officer Steele. "You weren't really supposed to get your arm stuck."

"No, sir, I know sir," mumbled Elvis.

"Keep still now, Elvis," reassured Sam. "We'll soon have you out of there."

And with a loud snap, the Jaws of Life cut through the metal. Elvis' arm was free!

James and Sarah arrived at the Fire Station on their skateboards. James was holding a football.

"Fancy a game of football, Uncle Sam?" asked James.

But before Sam could reply, Station Officer Steele shook his head.

"No football for your Uncle Sam today," he told the twins. "He is much too busy with this training exercise. Now off you both go and find something useful to do!"

"OK, we will!" said James. The twins jumped onto their skateboards and headed off.

Back at the Floods' house, Mike and Helen were talking about Mandy.

"She's very upset," sighed Helen. "I wish there was some way we could make it up to her."

Suddenly, Mike had the perfect plan to cheer up Mandy. "If we can't take Mandy to the carnival," he said, "why can't we bring the carnival to Mandy?"

Mike filled Helen in on his idea, then called Bella's café.

"Hello, Bella? Mike here," he said. "Do you know any Caribbean recipes? You do? Fantastic!"

Meanwhile, the twins were skateboarding through the village looking for something to do.

They turned a corner into an alley and skidded into a big pile of junk! There were burst bin bags, bits of broken furniture and even a battered old boiler.

"What a mess!" James said.

"I think we've found something useful to do," said Sarah. "Let's tidy up all this rubbish!"

James pulled at the pile of bin bags. Suddenly, the boiler on top of the rubbish started to wobble. It bounced down the bin bags, knocking James over!

"Ow!" cried James. "My leg is stuck under the boiler!"

Meanwhile, at Bella's café, Bella was busy stirring a big pot. She was making Caribbean rice and red beans for Mandy's Carnival.

Norman Price and Trevor Evans were also in the café, helping Bella get decorations ready for the party. Norman was twisting party balloons into animal shapes while Trevor supervised him.

"I want to make a dog like Dusty," said Norman, picking up a pink balloon.

Suddenly, Sarah burst into the café.

"Bella, can I use your phone?" asked Sarah.
"It's an emergency!"

"Mamma mia!" cried Bella. "Whasa happen?"

But there was no time to explain. Sarah picked up
the phone and dialled 999.

Over at the Fire Station, Penny received the call.
She quickly informed the other officers.

"Stand by, everybody," said Penny,
as the message came through.
"A boy is stuck under a boiler . . .
Oh no, it's James!"

"Action Stations!" called Station Officer Steele.

Sam and Elvis raced off in Jupiter. Penny was right behind them in Venus. **Nee Nah! Nee Nah!**

When they reached James, Dusty was looking after him.

"Keep calm, James," reassured Fireman Sam. "We'll have you out of here in no time!"

Carefully, Sam and Penny used the Jaws of Life to cut the boiler into smaller pieces. Soon James' leg was free!

"Stay clear of rubbish tips in future, James," said Sam. "They are full of hidden hazards."

Back at the Floods' house, Mandy was tucked up in bed reading a pony magazine.

She was feeling very sorry for herself.

"Oh, I wish we were going to the carnival in Jamaica!" sighed Mandy.

Suddenly, she heard steel band music coming from outside the front of the house.

"What's that?" Mandy puzzled.

Mandy got out of bed and went to the window to have a look.

As she looked out of her bedroom window, Mandy gasped in surprise: "Sam!"

Fireman Sam was on Jupiter's platform holding a bowl of Bella's Caribbean rice and red beans.

"Here you go, Mandy!" said Sam. "Something to cheer you up."

As Fireman Sam was lowered down, Mandy saw where the noise was coming from. Sam had made Mike a steel drum using the old boiler from the rubbish tip!

"Wow!" cried Mandy as her dad waved up at her.

As Mandy looked on, she saw palm trees and colourful balloons in her front garden. All her friends were there, waving and dancing!

Helen came into the room and joined Mandy at the window.

"It's just like the big carnival in Jamaica, Mum!" said Mandy.

"Yes, Mandy," smiled Helen. "You may have missed the carnival in Jamaica, but we have brought the Carnival to Pontypandy!"

"What are we waiting for?" said Mandy, happily. "Let's dance!"